D0908551

A Note to Parents and Caregivers:

Read-it! Readers are for children who are just starting on the amazing road to reading. These beautiful books support both the acquisition of reading skills and the love of books.

 The PURPLE LEVEL presents basic topics and objects using high frequency words and simple language patterns.

 The RED LEVEL presents familiar topics using common words and repeating sentence patterns.

 The BLUE LEVEL presents new ideas using a larger vocabulary and varied sentence structure.

 The YELLOW LEVEL presents more challenging ideas, a broad vocabulary, and wide variety in sentence structure.

 The GREEN LEVEL presents more complex ideas, an extended vocabulary range, and expanded language structures.

 The ORANGE LEVEL presents a wide range of ideas and concepts using challenging vocabulary and complex language structures.

When sharing a book with your child, read in short stretches, pausing often to talk about the pictures. Have your child turn the pages and point to the pictures and familiar words. And be sure to reread favorite stories or parts of stories.

There is no right or wrong way to share books with children. Find time to read with your child, and pass on the legacy of literacy.

Adria F. Klein, Ph.D.
Professor Emeritus
California State University
San Bernardino, California

Editor: Christianne Jones
Designer: Hilary Wacholtz
Art Director: Nathan Gassman
The illustrations in this book were created with watercolor and pencil.

Picture Window Books
A Capstone Imprint
151 Good Counsel Drive
P.O. Box 669
Mankato, MN 56002-0669
877-845-8392
www.capstonepub.com

Printed in the United States of America in Stevens Point, Wisconsin.
052010 005790R

Library of Congress Cataloging-in-Publication Data
Klein, Adria F. (Adria Fay), 1947-
Max goes to the nature center / by Adria F. Klein ; illustrated by
Mernie Gallagher-Cole.
p. cm. — (Read-it! readers. The life of Max)
ISBN 978-1-4048-5269-3 (hardcover)
[1. Nature centers—Fiction. 2. Hispanic Americans—Fiction.] I. Gallagher-Cole,
Mernie, ill. II. Title.
PZ7.K678324Maxn 2009
[E]—dc22
                                        2008030889

Max goes to the Nature Center

by Adria F. Klein
illustrated by Mernie Gallagher-Cole

Special thanks to our reading adviser:

Susan Kesselring, M.A., Literacy Educator
Rosemount–Apple Valley–Eagan (Minnesota) School District

PICTURE WINDOW BOOKS
Minneapolis, Minnesota

Zoe is going to the nature center.
She asks Max to go with her.

5

At the nature center, a sign has information about the animals.

The sign shows the colors and sizes of the animals. It shows how different animals live.

Max and Zoe go to see the snakes.
They see snakes of many colors.

They see snakes of different sizes.
The snakes are in many glass cages.

Max and Zoe see nests and holes where the snakes live.

They even see skin that the snakes
have shed.

Max and Zoe go to see the birds.
The birds are in a big cage.

Max and Zoe can go into the cage to see the different birds.

They see birds of many colors.
They see birds of different sizes.

They see many nests where the birds live.

They see five bird eggs and lots of feathers.

17

Max and Zoe go to the activity center. Max makes a paper snake.

Zoe makes a nest.

Max and Zoe want to see the
butterflies. But it is too late.
It is time to go home.

Outside, Max and Zoe see
butterflies everywhere.

Max and Zoe had fun at the
nature center.